This edition published by Parragon Books Ltd in 2015 and distributed by

Parragon Inc.
440 Park Avenue South, 13th Floor
New York, NY 10016
www.parragon.com

ISBN 978-1-4723-9632-7

Printed in China

Peter Pan

Read the story, then turn the book over
to read another story!

Bath • New York • Cologne • Melbourne • Delhi
Hong Kong • Shenzhen • Singapore • Amsterdam

There was once a house in London where Mr. and Mrs. Darling lived with their three children, Wendy, John, and Michael.

Watching over the children was Nana, the nursemaid, who also happened to be a dog. It was this home that Peter Pan liked to visit. He chose this house for one very special reason: there were people there who believed in him.

Wendy would tell stories
of Peter Pan and his adventures
in a magical place called
Never Land. Peter Pan loved
to sit in the shadows and listen.

One night, Peter and his fairy
friend, Tinker Bell, came back to
the nursery to find Peter's shadow.

Suddenly, Wendy woke up.
"Peter Pan!" she cried. "I knew
you'd come back!"

Wendy had been keeping
Peter's shadow safe. Carefully,
she sewed it back onto his feet.

Wendy explained to Peter that tonight was her last night in the nursery.

"I have to grow up tomorrow," she said.

"I won't have it!" Peter cried. "We're going to Never Land. You'll never grow up there!"

Wendy woke John and Michael so they could come, too.

"But Peter," said Wendy, "how do we get there?"

"Fly, of course!" answered Peter. He sprinkled the children with Tinker Bell's pixie dust and told them to think happy thoughts. Soon, they were flying out the window!

"We can fly!" shouted Wendy, John, and Michael as they soared through the skies with Peter and Tink. Finally, they spotted Never Land below them.

"There's a pirate ship!" cried Michael.

The captain of the pirate ship was Peter Pan's greatest enemy—Captain Hook!

"Blast that Peter Pan!" Hook said to his first mate, Mr. Smee. "If I could only find his hideout."

Captain Hook had got his name because he had a hook where his hand should have been. A crocodile had bitten it off long ago and was still after the rest of him! Luckily for Hook, there was an alarm clock in the crocodile's belly that went "tick-tock, tick-tock," so Hook could hear him coming.

Meanwhile, Peter Pan had taken Wendy to see the
Mermaid Lagoon. But John and Michael had no interest
in mermaids. They wanted an adventure with Peter's
friends, the Lost Boys!

"John, you be the leader," cried the Lost Boys. Then, they
lined up behind him and marched off into the forest. As John,
Michael, and the Lost Boys marched along, they made a plan.
They would be very clever and capture the Indians!

The plan might have worked, too, if the Indians hadn't caught them first! Michael and John were frightened until the Lost Boys explained that it was just a game—the Indians always let them go.

But this time the chief wouldn't set them free. He thought they had kidnapped his daughter, Tiger Lily!

Nearby, Peter Pan was showing Wendy the beautiful Mermaid Lagoon. Suddenly, he spotted Hook and Smee rowing a small boat—with Tiger Lily tied up in the back!

"It looks like they're headed for Skull Rock," Peter said. "Let's see what they're up to."

Captain Hook was threatening Tiger Lily. "If you don't tell me where Pan's hiding place is, I'll leave you here on the rock when the tide comes in!"

But Tiger Lily was a loyal friend and refused to give Peter away.

"I'll show the old codfish," Peter said as he set off to rescue Tiger Lily.

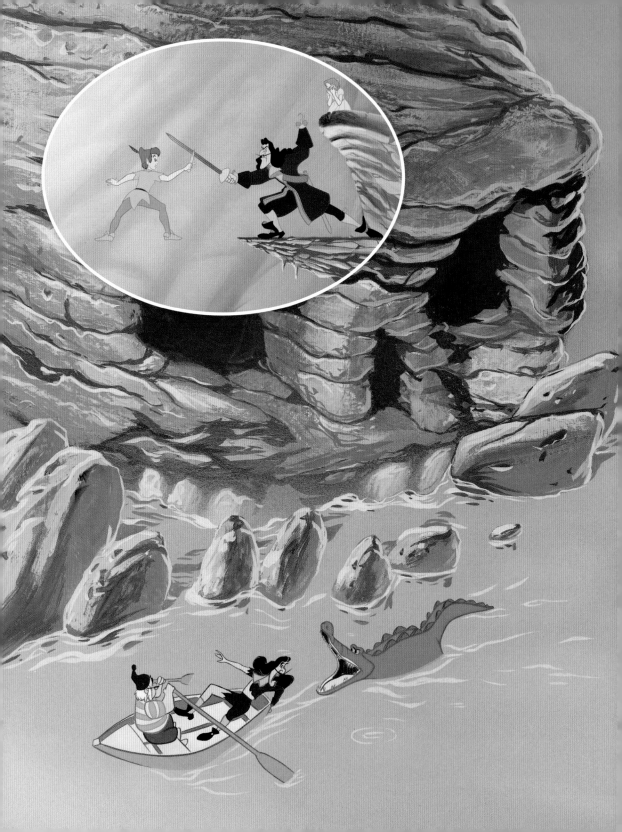

Peter Pan drew his sword and
fought Captain Hook. Wendy could
barely watch.

"I've got you this time, Pan!" cried Captain Hook,
forcing Peter near the edge of a cliff. But Peter danced out
of the way—into thin air!

When Captain Hook tried to catch Peter, he tumbled off
the cliff! Smee picked Captain Hook up in the rowboat, and the
crocodile began to chase them! While they rowed away, Peter
rescued Tiger Lily.

The Indian chief was so happy to see his daughter again that he freed John, Michael, and the Lost Boys. Then he placed a headdress of beautiful feathers on Peter Pan and proclaimed him "Chief Little Flying Eagle."

But not everyone wanted to join the celebration.
Back onboard his pirate ship, Captain Hook was
hatching an evil plot to get rid of Peter Pan.

Hook had lured jealous Tinker Bell into his lair and
promised that he would get rid of Wendy if she would
tell him where Peter's hideout was. But as soon as Tink
told him, he locked her in a glass lantern!

Meanwhile, at Peter's hideout, Wendy knew she and her brothers should go home soon. She sang about the wonders of a real mother until even the Lost Boys wanted to go to London! Only Peter wanted to stay.

One by one, the Lost Boys, Wendy, John, and Michael left the hideout—only to walk right into the arms of Hook's waiting pirates!

Captain Hook and his pirate gang led the prisoners away and tied them to the mast of his ship.

"I have left a little present for Peter," said Hook slyly to Smee. "It is due to blast off at six o'clock."

From her glass cage, Tinker Bell overheard Hook's plan. Hook had planted a bomb in Peter's hideout! Tink was furious. She knocked over the lantern and, with a CRACK, she was free.

Tinker Bell reached Peter's hideout just in
time—he was about to open the package!
There was no time to explain. Tink tried to pull
the package away, but it was too late. The box
began to smoke, until suddenly—KABOOM!

The explosion was so huge that it rocked Hook's ship! Captain Hook smiled. He had finally defeated his enemy!

"Join me or walk the plank!" Hook shouted.

"Join you? Never!" cried Wendy. She walked to the end of the plank and jumped. But there was no splash. . . .

Peter Pan had escaped the explosion and flown to Wendy's rescue! He set her down safely, then flew up onto the rigging. Hook scrambled up after him and drew his sword.

As Peter and Hook clashed swords, Wendy, Michael, John, and the Lost Boys battled it out with the other pirates.

Suddenly, Captain Hook lost his balance. He fell overboard and into the water, where a familiar crocodile was waiting. . . .

"Hooray for Captain Pan!" cried all the children.

"All right, ya swabs," said Peter, "let's cast off for London."

"Michael, John, we're going home!" smiled Wendy.

"Hoist the anchor!" cried Peter. "Tink, let's have some of your pixie dust!"

Tinker Bell flew around the ship, sprinkling her magical dust as she went. Then, up, up, up went the ship, and, as it rose, it began to glow like gold.

Back in London, Mrs. Darling found Wendy asleep by the window.

"Oh, Mother, we're back!" cried Wendy. While John and Michael slept, she told her parents all about her wonderful adventure in Never Land.

Suddenly, Mr. Darling noticed a ship made of clouds passing in front of the moon.

"You know," said Mr. Darling, "I have the strangest feeling I've seen that ship before. A long, long time ago."

And, indeed, he had.

The End

Now turn the book over
for another classic Disney tale!

PETER PAN
RETURN TO
NEVER·LAND

Now you've read the first Peter Pan
adventure, it's time to enjoy the second!

Bath · New York · Cologne · Melbourne · Delhi
Hong Kong · Shenzhen · Singapore · Amsterdam

High in the sky above London, Peter Pan and Tinker Bell
sailed off through the clouds to Never Land.

"Good-bye, Wendy!" Peter Pan shouted.

"I'll always believe in you, Peter Pan!" Wendy replied.

Wendy watched from her window as the pirate ship
disappeared into the distance. As she waved good-bye,
she wondered if she'd ever see her magical friends again.

It had been a long time since Wendy's adventures in Never Land. But she never stopped believing.

Years later, a grown-up Wendy still loved to tell stories of Peter Pan and the Lost Boys to her own children.

Her son, Danny, never got tired of hearing his mother's stories. He would sit on Wendy's knee and listen for hours.

But Wendy's daughter, Jane, didn't have time for childish stories of pirates and pixie dust. There was a war going on, and Jane had promised her father that she would take care of the family while he was away.

When Jane found out she and Danny had to go away somewhere safe until the war was over, she was furious.

"I'm not going!" Jane argued.

"We'll be together again soon," Wendy promised. "You must have faith, Jane."

"Faith, trust, and pixie dust!" Jane scoffed. "Those are just words from your stories. Peter Pan isn't real, and people don't fly!"

"You're lying. They are real!" yelled Danny. "One day I'll go to Never Land with Peter Pan and Tinker Bell, and you can't come!"

Danny stormed off and ran out of the room.

Jane felt guilty for upsetting Danny, but she still couldn't bring herself to believe in nonsense like Peter Pan. She curled up by the window and went to sleep.

Jane was fast asleep when, suddenly, a noise woke her
in the middle of the night. She gasped. Standing over her
was—could it be?—Captain Hook!

"Hello, Wendy," he said, mistaking Jane for her mother.
Before Jane could say a word, the pirates stuffed her
into a sack and jumped aboard Hook's flying pirate ship!

They set sail for the second star to the right and
straight on 'til morning—they were going to Never Land!

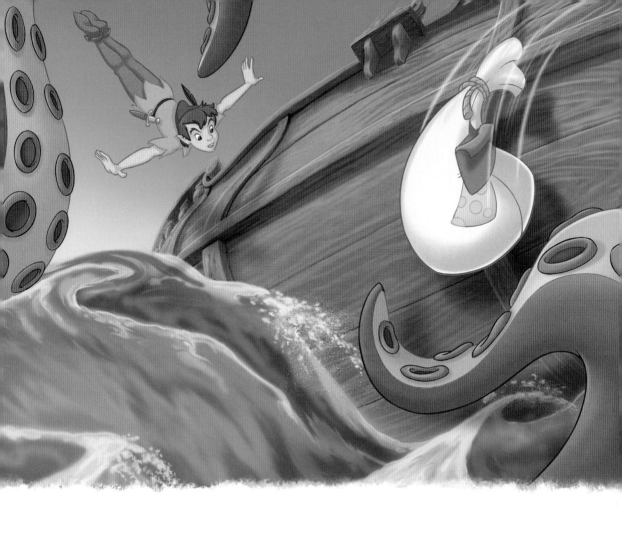

When they arrived in Never Land, Hook tried to use
Jane as bait to trap Peter Pan. He threw the sack with Jane
inside over the edge of the ship—right into the tentacles of
a giant, hungry octopus!

Suddenly, something dove into the water and caught
the sack just in time. It was Peter Pan!

Peter flew to a nearby rock and freed Jane from the sack. "You're sure not Wendy," he said, confused.

Jane gasped. Peter Pan and Tinker Bell were floating right before her eyes! Jane explained that she was Wendy's daughter. Peter could hardly believe it.

Peter Pan took Jane to meet the Lost Boys.

"Boys, this is Jane!" said Peter. "She's going to stay here and be our new mother and tell us stories."

Jane shook her head. "I'm afraid I'm not very good at telling stories," she said. "I have to go home."

The Lost Boys were disappointed and didn't understand why Jane wanted to leave.

"What's the matter with her?" they asked Peter.

"I don't know," said Peter. "She acts like . . . a grown-up!"

Later, Peter found Jane trying to build a raft. She was going to sail home!

"The only way out of here is to fly," he told her. "All it takes is faith, trust . . ."

"And pixie dust?" said Jane, unimpressed.

Peter took Jane back to the woods to see the Lost Boys and Tinker Bell.

"Look, anyone can do it," said Peter excitedly.
"Show her, Tink!"

Tinker Bell sprinkled pixie dust on the Lost Boys
and they began to fly! She then scattered lots of pixie
dust on Jane, too. But even with a good amount of
Tinker Bell's dust, Jane still couldn't fly.

Jane soon became frustrated with the Lost Boys'
silly games. She would never get home at this rate!

"I don't believe in any of this!" she cried, turning
to Tinker Bell. "And I especially don't believe in fairies!"

Peter, Tink, and the Lost Boys stood shocked as
Jane stormed off.

Suddenly, Tinker Bell's light began to fade. . . .

The boys gathered around Tinker Bell.

"If Jane doesn't believe in fairies, Tink's light will go out forever!" said Peter. "We've got to make her one of us, then she'll believe!"

Peter and the Lost Boys set out to look for Jane and help her believe.

But Captain Hook found Jane first. He promised to take her home on his pirate ship—on one condition.

"That pesky Peter Pan stole my treasure. If you help me to get it back, I'll take you straight home to London," he said slyly, handing Jane a whistle to blow when she found the treasure.

Jane agreed, as long as Hook promised not to hurt Peter or the Lost Boys.

The Lost Boys were happy to see Jane again. They took her on a wild adventure through Never Land.

Jane had so much fun that she forgot all about her responsibilities and being grown-up.

Peter told Jane they'd do anything for her.

"Why don't we play a game?" Jane suggested. "How about . . . a treasure hunt?"

Everyone started to search. Soon, Jane found herself in Dead Man's Cave. And there, right before her eyes, was Hook's treasure!

Peter Pan was so impressed that Jane had found the treasure, he proclaimed her the very first Lost Girl. Jane was honored. She threw the whistle away and decided she would never tell Hook about the treasure.

But one of the Lost Boys found the whistle—and he blew it!

Hook and his pirates swooped into the cave and captured Peter and his gang.

Peter thought Jane had betrayed them. "You lied to me!" he cried. "And because you don't believe in fairies, Tink's light is going out!"

Jane felt horrible. Peter and his friends were in trouble and it was all her fault.

There wasn't a moment to lose! Jane ran as fast as she could back to Tinker Bell's house.

When Jane found her, Tinker Bell's light had almost faded to nothing.

"This is all my fault," Jane sobbed. "I'm so sorry, Tink!"

Suddenly, Tinker Bell's light began to flicker back to life. Jane did believe!

On Hook's pirate ship, the Lost Boys stood chained to the mast. And Captain Hook was about to make Peter Pan walk the plank!

"Say your prayers, Peter Pan!" said Hook with an evil laugh.

"Not so fast, you old codfish!" said a voice. It was Jane—and Tinker Bell was at her side!

"Jane!" cried Peter. "Tinker Bell, you're alive!"

Jane snatched the key from Hook and freed Peter and the Lost Boys. An angry Captain Hook chased her up the mast.

"Give up, girl!" Captain Hook snarled.

"Never!" cried Jane. And thanks to a little faith, trust, and pixie dust, she jumped off the mast and flew right out of Hook's grasp! When Hook tried to reach her, he tumbled overboard and into the ocean!

Meanwhile, the Lost Boys had been throwing Hook's treasure into the ocean—and the pirates were jumping in after it!

Soon, the pirates and their captain were being chased through the ocean by the giant, hungry octopus.

The Lost Boys—and Girl—had defeated Captain Hook! The pirates were gone and everyone was safe.

Before long, Peter, Tink, and Jane were flying over Never Land and back home to London.

Back home, Danny listened intently as Jane told him all about her adventures with Peter Pan in Never Land.

Wendy peered out the window as she listened to Jane's stories. "Peter?" she whispered. And there he was.

"You've changed," said Peter curiously.

"Not really," Wendy replied. "Not ever."

Suddenly, there was a knock at the door. Jane's father was finally home! As the happy family reunited, Peter and Tink flew off to the second star on the right and straight on 'til morning.

Jane ran to the window and made a promise, "I'll always believe in you, Peter Pan."

The End

Now turn the book over to
enjoy the adventure again!